Library
Library
HABERDASHERS' GIRLS JNR
R16325F3034
D1394747

For the children of Waverley Primary School
G.S.

To Paula, Emily, Eunice
and all the other children who love reading books
with all my affection.
F.C.

First published in Great Britain in 2011 by
Gullane Children's Books
185 Fleet Street, London, EC4A 2HS
www.gullanebooks.com

10   9   8   7   6   5   4   3   2   1

Text © Gillian Shields 2011
Illustrations © Francesca Chessa 2011

The right of Gillian Shields and Francesca Chessa to be identified as the author and illustrator of
this work has been asserted by them in accordance with the Copyright, Designs and Patents Act, 1988.
A CIP record for this title is available from the British Library.

ISBN: 978-1-86233-830-2

All rights reserved. No part of this publication may be reproduced, stored in a retrieval system, or transmitted
in any form or by any means electronic, mechanical, photocopying, recording or otherwise, without prior permission.

Printed and bound in China

Library
Lily

Gillian Shields

illustrated by
Francesca
Chessa

GULLANE
CHILDREN'S BOOKS

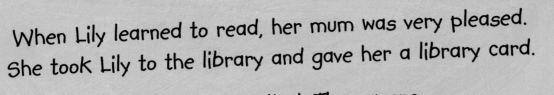

When Lily learned to read, her mum was very pleased.
She took Lily to the library and gave her a library card.

Lily was so excited. There were
fat books, thin books, enormous great square books,
old books, new books and furry-touchy-feely books.

Going to the library was like going on an adventure.

THIS WAY

MY LITTLE DOG BOOK

MY BIG CAT BOOK

Lily's library card

The trouble was, once Lily started to read, she couldn't stop.

She read at night
under the bed clothes.
...and the purple spotted
sea monster rose up
from the waves...

"Lily!" said Mum.
"Aren't you asleep yet?!"

She read in the
morning when she was
brushing her teeth.
...the rare stripy
Amazonian snake
lays its eggs...

"I need the bathroom, Lily!"

When her dinner was
ready, she forgot to eat.
...until that moment, I,
Herbert Wobble-Smythe,
had never seen a ghost...

"Lily, please eat up!"

And when her mum
spoke to her,
she just didn't hear.
...long, long ago, far,
far away, there was
once a perfect...

"Oh, Lily . . ." laughed Mum.

Lily read and read and read.

"There goes Library Lily,"
people began to say.
"Always got her head in a book."

Lily read all the way through a sizzling summer . . .

an awesome autumn . . .

a wonderful winter.

And when spring came round again . . .

she didn't notice.
She was in a beautiful dream. She was reading.

One sunny morning,
Lily's mum took her to the park.
"Why don't you go and play?" Mum asked.

"But I want to finish my story," said Lily.
"It's such an exciting adventure."
"Maybe you'll have an adventure in the park" smiled Mum.

So Lily mooched over to the playground...

WELCOME TO THE PARK

and read the notices.

That didn't take long.

She was just wondering what else she could
find to read, when someone called out . . .

"Hey! What are you doing?"
"Reading, of course!" said Lily.
"Reading's boring!" said the upside-down voice.
"In fact, I hate reading."

"Hate reading!" gasped Lily.
"What DO you like?"

"Lots of things!" the upside-down person said.
"Playing. Climbing. Exploring . . .

"I'm Milly," said Milly.
"I'm Lily," said Lily.

Milly grinned.
"Would you like to climb my tree?"

Lily scrambled up the tree to join Milly.
From the top, they could see the green park, the busy streets,
the library and the town, all spread out below them like a picture.
"Wow!" said Lily.

"There's a whole world out there," said Milly.
"There's a whole world in here too,"
said Lily, pulling a book from her bag.

"You'll see!"

And so, all summer long,
Milly took Lily exploring.
It was fun!

Lily took Milly on adventures too.
Milly decided that books weren't boring.
They were great!

And what was extra-special
was doing everything **together!**

"There goes Library Lily,"
people began to say.
"With her best friend

Milly."

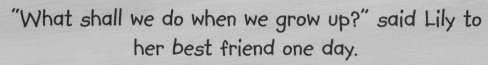

"What shall we do when we grow up?" said Lily to
her best friend one day.

"Be explorers!" said Milly.
"There's a WHOLE WORLD out there."

So that's exactly what they did.

And when they came home again,
Lily wrote down all their adventures...

... in the most
marvellous, magical, amazing,
PERFECT BOOK!
(You might just find it in your library!)